Fashion Fairy Princess

With fairy big thanks to Catherine Coe

First published in the UK in 2014 by Scholastic Children's Books
An imprint of Scholastic Ltd
Euston House, 24 Eversholt Street
London, NW1 1DB, UK
Registered office: Westfield Road, Southam, Warwickshire, CV47 0RA
SCHOLASTIC and associated logos are trademarks and/or registered
trademarks of Scholastic Inc.

Text copyright © Scholastic Ltd, 2014
Cover copyright © Pixie Potts, Beehive Illustration Agency, 2014
Inside illustration copyright © David Shephard, The Bright Agency, 2014

The right of Poppy Collins to be identified as the author
of this work has been asserted by her.

ISBN 978 1407 13958 6

A CIP catalogue record for this book is available from the British Library.

Printed and bound by CPI Group (UK) Ltd, Croydon, CR0 4YY
Papers used by Scholastic Children's Books are made
from wood grown in sustainable forests.

3 5 7 9 10 8 6 4 2

This is a work of fiction. Names, characters, places,
incidents and dialogues are products of the author's imagination
or are used fictitiously. Any resemblance to actual people, living
or dead, events or locales is entirely coincidental.

www.scholastic.co.uk
www.fashionfairyprincess.com

Fashion Fairy Princess

Honey

❀ in Shimmer Island ❀

POPPY COLLINS

◼SCHOLASTIC

Dream
Mountain

Jewel Forest

Sparkle
City

Star
Valley

River
Sapphire

Shimmer Island

Glitter Ocean

Welcome to the world of the
fashion fairy princesses! Join Honey
and friends on their magical adventures
in fairyland.

They can't wait to visit

Shimmer Island!

Can you?

Chapter 1

"How about we go shopping?" Violet suggested. She sat cross-legged on Bluebell's rug, fiddling with the petal tassels.

"I suppose we could," said Bluebell, who lay on her giant four-poster bed, flicking through fashion magazines.

Buttercup looked up from Bluebell's mussel-shell dressing table, where she was picking out a nail varnish to go with her bright-yellow cardigan. "But shopping's not the same without Rosa," she said. "I really miss her."

It was the start of the summer holidays, and Rosa had gone to stay with her cousin Honey on Shimmer Island. The beginning of the summer holidays was always an exciting time — long, sunny days stretched out ahead of them, ready to be filled with fun, adventures and fashion! But it felt strange without Rosa, and the three remaining best friends were finding it hard to get excited about anything.

"What's that noise?" Buttercup asked all of a sudden. She tucked her long blonde hair behind her little ears and listened harder. She was sure she could hear something humming!

"Oh, look!" cried Violet. She rushed over to Bluebell's star-shaped window and opened it wide, and a beautiful blue and green hummingbird darted into the room. It fluttered over to land on Bluebell's dressing table and hummed a low, gentle melody.

"What's that in its beak?" Buttercup

asked. She moved her hand towards the bird, taking care not to frighten it, and cupped her palm in front of its beak.

Bluebell smiled – Buttercup was always so gentle with animals. She seemed to have a special kind of bond with them.

The bird stopped humming, just for a moment, and dropped something into Buttercup's hand. Then it gave a quick flutter of its pretty blue wings and rose up and back out of the window.

The three fairy princesses took a moment to watch it fly away – they didn't see many of these stunning birds in Sparkle City. Most of them lived out in the trees of Jewel Forest.

Violet leaned over Buttercup. "So, what is it?" She peered into Buttercup's hands, her long curly hair falling on to her face.

"It's an envelope – I wonder what's inside!" Buttercup said. She began to open it, and pulled out a little sparkling postcard, with looping swirls of handwriting across it. Buttercup read out the message in her soft, quiet voice.

Dear Violet, Buttercup and Bluebell,

Please come and join our holiday on Shimmer Island.

It's beautiful here, but we miss you!

Don't forget to pack your summer outfits. . .

The royal butterflies are waiting for you outside!

Lots of love, Honey and Rosa xxx

"Oh my fairyness!" cried Violet. "I've never been to Shimmer Island before, but it sounds amazing!" The island was a long way away from Sparkle City, past Star Valley and River Sapphire, and right in the middle of Glitter Ocean.

"And we're to go right away?" said Bluebell, already fluttering across her bedroom, pulling out her suitcase and flinging it open.

Buttercup was looking out of Bluebell's window at the courtyard below. "Yes — the butterflies really are waiting for us outside!" she said. "I'd better get packing." She flew over to the door and zoomed out into the white marble hallway of Glimmershine Palace.

Violet was close behind her. "See you downstairs in ten ticks of a dandelion clock!" she called to Bluebell as she flew out of the bedroom.

The fashion fairy princesses packed as quickly as they could. They couldn't wait to get to Shimmer Island to join Rosa on her holiday. Bluebell pulled out her lavender-petal swimsuit with matching sarong from her pearl chest of drawers, and then she fluttered to her giant fly-in wardrobe on the other side of her room. She spun round, looking for

the perfect outfits to take on a summer
holiday, and found a gorgeous silk top in
a shimmering indigo blue, and a sky-blue
cotton summer dress with pretty
lace sleeves.

Meanwhile, Buttercup was flicking
through the clothes in her fly-in wardrobe,
wondering what to take and what to leave

behind. Her spider's-web skirt with glitter belt? Yes! Her lemon-yellow wrap dress with gold trim? Yes! And what about her daisy-chain sandals, her wide-brimmed summer hat, and her shell-string necklace? Yes, yes, yes! She just hoped her suitcase was big enough. . .

In her bedroom, Violet had almost finished packing. She folded her palm-leaf cape at the top of her glittery lilac suitcase. "Done!" she said to herself as she clicked the clasps shut. She grabbed the handle, but when she tried to flutter up with it, she found she couldn't move! *Oops.* She knew she had packed too much, but she had to get going – the butterflies, and Rosa and Honey, were waiting!

"We can help you with that," came two small, high voices behind her.

Violet turned round and beamed. At her
door stood two tiny fairy-helpers. There
were lots of these helpers at Glimmershine
Palace — they assisted the fairies with daily
tasks and errands. Even though they were
only half Violet's height, their double wings
meant they were super strong and very fast.

"Oh, thank you!" Violet replied, as the two helpers picked up her suitcase between them and zoomed as fast as dragonflies along the palace's hallway and down the glass staircase.

Violet flew off behind them, and was soon rushing out on to the palace's sweeping pathway, where three royal butterflies with enormous deep purple wings waited patiently on the stones. Buttercup and Bluebell were already sitting on their butterflies' backs, grinning. Violet fluttered up to the remaining butterfly and nestled herself between the butterfly's soft purple wings.

Bluebell's blue eyes sparkled with excitement. "All ready?" she said, as Violet and Buttercup nodded their heads. "Shimmer Island, here we come!"

Chapter 2

The fairy princesses loved flying by themselves, but there was something extra special about being aboard a royal butterfly. The great wings were so powerful that they could fly much faster than a fairy – or even a winged pony – and their strong legs carried the suitcases with ease. The wind whipped through Buttercup's blonde hair as they rose higher and higher. It was a perfect

summer's day, warm but not too hot, with not one cloud in the bright blue sky.

"There's Star Valley!" shouted Violet, pointing down at the rolling green hills and sparkling stream. "Can you see Fern?"

Fern was a star fairy, and a very good friend of the fashion fairy princesses. Star Valley wasn't far from Sparkle City, so they often visited each other, especially in the holidays.

Bluebell shook her head. "We're so high up, all I can see are dots!" she said.

They were flying over River Sapphire now, and Bluebell was leaning forward, trying to stretch her head over her butterfly's wings. "I'm watching out for Glitter Ocean!" she explained. "I can't wait to see the gorgeous sparkling sea."

"Please be careful!" said Buttercup. Bluebell could be really clumsy sometimes, and Buttercup didn't want her to fall off her butterfly from all the way up here!

Suddenly Glitter Ocean came into view, and Buttercup couldn't help but gasp. The sea was a deep turquoise blue, and she could see how it got its name – it glittered like a giant jewel as the sun's rays bounced off it.

The three fairies stared out ahead of them, but all they could see was water. Violet was starting to wonder just how far away the island was.

But then they saw something glimmer like a tiny diamond on the horizon.

"Is that Shimmer Island?" Violet asked.

But her two friends didn't need to reply. The butterflies were flying so quickly that they could soon make out a moon-shaped island, surrounded by silver sand and covered in bright green palm trees. As they got closer, they could hear a beautiful sound ringing out across the island.

"Songbirds!" Buttercup realized. "I heard that there are thousands of them living in

the palm trees on Shimmer Island! Don't they sound magical?"

The fairy princesses took in the stunning view as the butterflies slowed down to land on the shore of the island. The sand really was sparkling – Buttercup spotted tiny crystals in among the sand grains – and the tall emerald-green palm trees looked beautiful against the bright blue sky. As the three friends fluttered down from the royal butterflies, they heard a shout.

"Oh, Violet, Buttercup, Bluebell, it *is* you! I'm so glad you came!" It was Rosa, her pink wings shaking with joy as she flew like a shooting star to greet them. She was wearing a flowing cream maxi-dress with a crown of pale pink flowers in her long dark hair and already looked at home on the island.

Then came Honey, skipping over the sand in a gorgeous turquoise grass skirt,

her thick blonde
plait waving
behind her.
"You made it!"
she said in her
sing-song voice.
"Welcome to
Shimmer Island!"

Rosa was
already reaching
out to Buttercup,
Violet and
Bluebell to give
them a group hug.
"I think you'll love
it here!" she cried. "I missed
you so much, and as soon as I told
Honey she suggested inviting you right
away!"

"The more the merrier!" said Honey

as the royal butterflies took off from the beach. "Now come on, I want to show you the *whole* island!"

Rosa looked down at her friends' bulging suitcases. "Maybe we should go and unpack first."

Violet grinned – super-organized Rosa did seem a lot more laid-back here, but she would always be the practical one!

Honey widened her big brown eyes at her cousin. "Oh please, Rosa, we can unpack later. There'll be plenty of time for that!"

Rosa looked at her fairy princess friends, their faces alight with excitement. "Oh, all right then," she gave in. "There *are* lots of amazing things to show you!"

"First stop, the Sand Castle!" cried Honey.

Buttercup glanced at Bluebell. A

sandcastle didn't sound all that amazing, but they followed Honey anyway as she flew in and out of the palm trees. It was nice and cool under the shade of the big leaves. Soon they emerged at a different part of the beach, which Honey said was called Golden Bay, and Buttercup couldn't help her jaw dropping when she saw just what Honey had meant by "the sandcastle".

"Wow!" Violet darted ahead to get a closer look.

In front of them stood a castle almost as big as Glimmershine Palace. It was made of the same crystal sand that was on the beach, which made it sparkle like a diamond in the sun.

"That's my bedroom," said Honey, pointing to a circular turret that rose up high into the sky. "You'll all be staying

with me, like a proper sleepover. I'll show you inside the castle later. Next stop, the waterfall!"

Honey zoomed off over the tops of the palm trees, the four fashion fairy princesses following close behind. She led them to the other end of the island and fluttered down in a small clearing. Before they had even landed, the fairies were hit by the most delicious smell. Gorgeous aromas of honeysuckle and jasmine and roses and sweet peas filled the air.

As they drew in deep breaths, Honey beckoned them down to a rushing waterfall. "It's scented," she explained, "by all the flowers around it."

The friends gazed at the waterfall that poured from a high ledge. It was surrounded by flowers of every shape and colour imaginable. The water seemed to release the flowers' scents as it splashed down to join a river that weaved away towards the sea.

"This is the Forever Happy Waterfall," explained Honey. "It's said to be enchanted – the longer you spend breathing in the flowers' sweet perfume, the happier you'll be."

"Oh, it looks very magical," said Violet, although she wasn't sure that she needed

the help of the waterfall – she was already
very happy!

Honey grinned. "There'll be lots
of time to come back here," she said,
looking up at the midday sun. "As it's
getting hotter, there's somewhere else we
should go next."

As they flew up and over the palm trees once more, Bluebell wondered where they were heading. The island seemed like a wonderful place. Bluebell was so happy they were going to be spending their holidays here!

"That's where the sand fairies live." Rosa pointed down at a cove where little houses dotted the shore. "Their homes are pretty huts made of coconut shells!"

But they weren't stopping here – Honey dashed ahead.

"Not much further!" Honey called back over her shoulder. "I promise you, it'll be worth it!"

Chapter 3

Suddenly Honey dived down past the
canopy of palm trees. She pushed back
layers of lush plants so that her friends
could fly through. Underneath, her surprise
revealed itself. Hidden away beneath
the plants, a large natural pool glistened,
surrounded by flower-covered rocks.

As soon as she saw it, Violet wanted to
dive straight in! It looked so refreshing.

"It's *always* so sunny on Shimmer Island, and this is one of my favourite places to come when it's a bit too hot," Honey explained. "I know we're not wearing our swimming costumes, but we can float out on these lily pads. I promise you, you'll love it!" She knelt down beside the edge of the pool and began fishing out lily pads and passing them around.

Violet had already taken off her lilac pumps and tied back her curly hair so it didn't get wet. Rosa laughed as Violet slid tummy down on to her lily pad,

paddling with her arms and legs out into the middle of the pool. She made it look very easy, but Rosa was a bit worried about falling off!

Honey noticed Rosa's concern, and fluttered over to put an arm around her cousin. "It's OK – these are very special lily pads," she said. "No matter how much you tilt them, you can't fall in!"

That made Rosa feel a lot better. Soon she had joined her friends, and was splashing around the pool. Feeling the water flow past her hands and feet was *so* cooling, and the palm trees that bent over the pool shaded them from the hot sun. *It's a bit like floating on a cloud*, Rosa thought, swimming about gently while listening to the laughter of her friends.

"Now it *really* feels like a holiday," said Bluebell as she paddled with just one

hand to spin herself round and round. "Oops, sorry, Buttercup!" she added, when she realized she'd splashed her friend with the spray. Buttercup grinned to show she wasn't really annoyed.

"I'm glad you're having fun, Bluebell," said Honey. Then she winked. "But the best is yet to come — just you wait and see!"

The five friends spent the whole afternoon

at the pool, eating cucumber-star salads for lunch and drinking coconut milk straight from the nut. But by the time the sun started to set over the horizon, Honey still hadn't told them the plan, although no one was very surprised – Honey was so easy-going about everything!

"I suppose we should go back to the Sand Castle now," said Honey, as the setting sun cast a beautiful red glow over the whole island. "We need to get ready for this evening."

"What do we need to get ready for?" Rosa asked.

But Honey put her finger to her lips and shook her head. "I can't say – not yet. . ."

The fairy princesses flew back over the island's palm trees towards the sparkling castle in Golden Bay. Honey led them to the main door, where the sand had been

shaped like two mermaids, each side of
the door. But even though the outside
of the castle was all sand, inside was a
different matter. Shell tiles covered every
single surface. On the floor were flat
scallop shells, while the walls and ceilings
were made of beautiful pearl shells.

Buttercup loved the tinkling sound
their feet made on the shell tiles as they
skipped into the entrance hall. They
fluttered up a wide spiral staircase, and

soon they were all flopping down on Honey's huge seaweed hammock-bed. It was so big that all five of them could fit in at once!

But they didn't rest for long. Rosa was the first to get up and sit at Honey's starfish dressing table, combing through her long hair with a brush made from a beautiful pink shell. "Should we put on some nice clothes, Honey?" she asked. She didn't want to spoil the surprise, but she wanted to be prepared!

"Oh yes, definitely," Honey answered, jumping out of the hammock and fluttering into her dressing room. The fairy princesses grinned at one another when they heard Honey singing as she looked for something to wear. *"Now the fairy princesses are here, let's all sing and dance and cheer!"*

One thing was for sure: Honey was a

very happy fairy to be around!

Honey's bedroom soon turned into a hive of activity as Violet, Buttercup and Bluebell began digging through their suitcases. Flip-flops, sunglasses and hats went flying as they each searched for the perfect outfit for that night. Rosa quickly gave up trying to tidy everything away, and helped her friends instead.

She had already put on a gorgeous pink

linen dress. "Perfect for a hot summer evening!" she said.

Violet finally found the lilac strapless dress that she'd been looking for.

"Ooh, I have a lovely hairband that would match your dress," said Rosa. "Would you like to borrow it?"

"Yes, please!" Violet beamed, and slid the jewel-studded hairband over her head, pulling her thick hair back from her face. Even though the sun had set, it was still warm outside and she didn't want to get too hot.

Bluebell chose her indigo silk top, with pale-blue sequinned shorts. She was delighted when Honey asked if she'd liked to borrow her silver wedge sandals. The wedges were the perfect shoes for her outfit! Meanwhile, Buttercup made her decision easily – she'd been desperate to

wear her glitter belt ever since she'd bought
it from Sparkle Sensations last week. She
tucked a yellow blouse into it and added
gold pointy pumps.

"Oh, you all look gorgeous!" said
Honey, fluttering about wearing gold-silk
cropped trousers and a white vest top. "So,
are you ready?"

The fairy princesses nodded at once.
"YES!" they all shouted. They couldn't
wait to find out Honey's big surprise!

Chapter 4

Rosa could hardly believe her eyes when she stepped out of the door of the Sand Castle. It was night-time, but the beach was brightly lit by hundreds of moon-shaped lanterns hanging from the palm trees. The sand sparkled more than ever, and the air was filled with the sound of songbirds chirping an upbeat melody.

"Surprise!" Suddenly hundreds of

blonde-haired sand fairies fluttered out
from behind the palm trees, waving and
smiling. They all wore grass skirts in
different colours, and had beautiful flower
garlands around their necks.

The fashion fairy princesses were lost
for words – even Violet! It was such a
spectacular and unexpected sight that

Bluebell couldn't help but squeeze Rosa's hand in excitement.

"We wanted to do something to welcome you all to the island," explained Honey. "So we decided to do what we do best — throw a party!"

Two sand fairies flew towards them, holding piles of flowers in their hands. When they got closer, Violet realized they weren't just flowers, but flower garlands, just like the ones the sand fairies were wearing.

"Hello! I'm Luna, and this is Chelle," said a sand fairy with bobbed blonde hair. "We made these for you."

"Have we got the colours right?" Chelle asked. She had a crown of palm leaves nestled on top of her golden locks.

"Oh yes!" said Violet, finally managing to speak. The garlands were in each of the fairy princesses' favourite colours. She plucked the purple garland from the pile and popped it carefully over her head. "Thank you," she said, grinning. "It's *so* pretty!"

"Yes, thank you!" said the other fairy princesses. Rosa picked up the bright pink garland, Buttercup the golden-yellow one and Bluebell took the garland of delicate sky-blue flowers. Then Luna and Chelle pinned a few tropical flowers in each of the fairy princesses' hair.

Honey turned to them and clapped her hands. "Now you're wearing everything you need for a Shimmer Island party, it's time to dance!" She flew off towards the sea, where a circular dance floor made of woven seaweed was lit up next to the shoreline. Beside it, a row of red crabs clacked their claws in time to the music. Honey fluttered on to the dance floor, and as soon as her feet touched it, it began to move slowly clockwise.

"You've got to come and join in!" Honey called, and Violet and Rosa flew over immediately.

Rosa began skipping about and fluttering her wings to the beat, and the spinning dance floor felt as though it was moving in time to the music! When the music became slower, the dance floor would slow down, and when the melody quickened, the dance floor would suddenly speed up. "Oh my fairyness!" said Rosa. "This is so much fun!"

But Bluebell noticed that Buttercup was standing, frozen, on the glistening sand. "Don't you want to dance?" she asked, frowning at her friend.

Buttercup looked up shyly. "I do," she said, "very much. But I'm not sure I can with everyone watching. . ."

Bluebell glanced around. Buttercup was right — most of the sand fairies

had circled the dance floor, and were clapping their hands as Violet, Rosa and Honey danced about with big smiles on their faces. Bluebell knew how shy Buttercup could be, especially around fairies she didn't know. Of course she was worried about dancing in front of everyone. Bluebell looked about at all the sand fairies, clapping as they watched her friends dance. Suddenly she had an idea.

She jumped on to the dance floor. "How about a conga?" she cried, and the songbirds immediately changed their song to a two-beat rhythm. Bluebell took the lead, and the sand fairies poured on to the dance floor, lining up behind each other and kicking out their legs in time to the music. Fluttering their wings, they flew back and forth and upwards and downwards across the seaweed dance

floor. A warm wave of happiness washed through Bluebell when she saw that Buttercup had joined the conga, and was shaking her hips towards the back of the line. Now *everyone* was dancing.

As Bluebell brought the conga to an end, a sound quite different from the songbirds' melody started up – a gentle tapping rhythm that was becoming louder and louder. Rosa swung round, trying to work out exactly where it was coming from.

"Wow!" Rosa gasped when she saw the procession of sand fairies fluttering out from behind the Sand Castle. The fairies all had different-sized shell drums hung around their necks, and they tapped out a fun, magical tune.

"We *must* dance to this!" cried Honey, grabbing the hands of Buttercup and Rosa. Bluebell glanced at Buttercup, worried that she'd still be feeling shy, but instead she was the first to start dancing! Soon, they were all doing twirls in the air together.

Honey showed the fairy princesses how to do a triple high-kick spin. It wasn't long before they got the hang of it, and they danced and spun together in the sparkling Golden Bay air.

"This is wonderful!" cried Buttercup, laughing with delight.

The fairy princesses had so much fun

dancing that the evening whizzed by much too fast. They couldn't believe it when the sand-fairy drummers lowered their shell drums and began to proceed away. It was time for bed!

As Violet fell into Honey's hammock-bed with her friends, she realized just how exhausted she was. She barely had time to wonder what the fun-loving Honey had in store for them tomorrow

before her eyes closed, the hammock
gently rocking the friends to sleep.

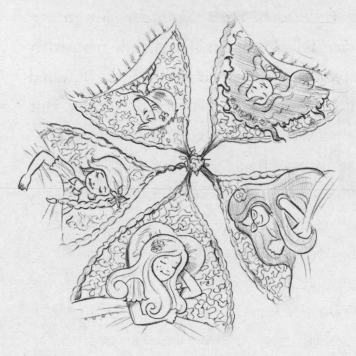

✦

Rosa stretched up her arms and yawned.
It took a moment to remember where
she was, and then she sighed happily –
they were on holiday on Shimmer Island!
She climbed out of the hammock-bed,

taking care not to wake her friends, who were all still curled up asleep. Honey was nowhere to be seen. *She must have got up earlier*, Rosa thought. Rosa didn't want to disturb the others, so she silently fluttered out to Honey's shell-covered balcony. But the view was so different from yesterday that she reached up to her face to check that she had her glasses on. Yes, her pretty dark-rimmed frames were in place – so what was going on outside?

The sky was an awful dark grey, instead of its usual bright blue, and the beach was a dull grey too. It was as if Shimmer

Island had been covered in a horrible dirty blanket. Rosa could see lots of sand fairies rushing about on the shore of Golden Bay with frowns on their faces, rubbing their arms to keep warm. *What in fairyland has happened?* thought Rosa.

Just then her friends began to stir.

"Good morning, Rosa," said Buttercup, as she rubbed the sleep from her eyes.

"I'm afraid this morning doesn't seem very good at all," said Rosa. "Look outside!"

The fairy princesses jumped up and flew to the window.

"Perhaps it's just a passing storm?" Bluebell suggested.

"But didn't Honey say that Shimmer Island is *always* sunny?" said Violet. "It looks like something really bad has happened!"

Chapter 5

"Let's go downstairs to breakfast and see what's going on," Rosa suggested.

"Good idea," replied Violet, and the four fashion fairy princesses began to get dressed quickly.

As she added an acorn-nut slide to her blonde hair, Buttercup looked down at her lemon-yellow wrap dress sadly. "Oh dear – our summer clothes seem really out of place now it's all grey and miserable outside."

"You're right," Bluebell agreed, staring at her sky-blue skirt in the mirror. "But we don't have anything else to wear!"

The four best friends zoomed out of Honey's bedroom and down the spiral stairs, almost crashing into Honey at the bottom.

"I was just coming to get you," Honey explained. "There's been a bit of a disaster here on Shimmer Island. . ."

"Has it got something to do with the grey skies?" asked Rosa as she and her friends fluttered down the last few steps to join Honey.

"I'm afraid so," said Honey. "We've run out of sunshine!"

Violet creased up her face in confusion. "What do you mean, run out?"

"Well, Shimmer Island is kept sunny all year round because we are given bottles

of sunshine by the sky fairies. We store them behind the waterfall — you know, the one I took you to yesterday?"

"Forever Happy Waterfall?" Buttercup put in.

"Yes, that's the one," Honey replied. "But the problem is, the reserve bottles of sunshine have gone missing! Without them, Shimmer Island will stay grey and miserable. What are we going to do?"

The fairy princesses shared a worried look.

"Perhaps we can help?" Bluebell suggested. "Do you have any idea where the sunshine bottles might have gone?"

Honey shook her head. "No idea," she said. "But they've never disappeared before, so I'm worried that they've been stolen."

"But who would do such a thing?" said Rosa, shocked that there might be a thief on beautiful Shimmer Island.

Violet's forehead wrinkled with a determined frown. "I have no idea," she said, "but we're going to find out!" With that, she flew out of the Sand Castle, her friends following her close behind.

The sight outside was so dreadful that Buttercup felt tears pricking her eyes. The sand on the shore of Golden Bay had lost its sparkle, the palm trees drooped like rag dolls, and the ocean looked grey and uninviting. Most horrible of all was the silence — not one of the songbirds was singing, which was very strange indeed for an island usually full of music. It was hard to believe that it was the same place where they'd had the magical party last night!

Sand fairies rushed around, talking in worried tones. They seemed so different from their usual happy selves. Luna and Chelle flew by in a hurry, giving them sad little waves as they passed.

"Everyone's been looking ever since dawn," said Honey. "But so far nothing's been found."

The friends all stood on the sand, not sure where to start. All except Rosa, that is, who had begun drawing lines in the sand with a large conch shell. "So we're here," she said, pointing to a place in the sand she'd marked with a cross, "and the waterfall is all the way over there."

Bluebell fluttered closer to her friend to see what Rosa was doing. She'd sketched out the moon shape of Shimmer Island in the sand, with Golden Bay at the top and the Forever Happy Waterfall at the very bottom. In the middle of the circle she'd drawn the pool, and a little further down,

the sand fairies' coconut beach huts.

"Let's start by searching the north of the island," Rosa said. "Honey, can you think of anywhere the bottles of sunshine might be hidden?"

Honey raised her eyes in thought for a moment. "We could try the palm trees behind the castle? There are so many, the bottles of sunshine could easily be hidden among them."

"Good idea!" said Violet, and the fairies flew off at once, weaving through the hundreds of tall palm trees that stood at the rear of the Sand Castle.

They looked around the trunks of the trees and beneath fallen leaves. But everything seemed so miserable in the grey morning — it didn't seem as if the magical sunshine was close by. The fairies even fluttered up to the drooping treetops to look between the palms and coconuts, but they couldn't find the bottles anywhere.

"It's like looking for fairy-dust in a sandcastle – impossible!" Bluebell exclaimed. "What are we going to do?"

Chapter 6

"Let's not panic," said Rosa, fluttering back to the map of Shimmer Island she'd drawn in the sand. "I think we should try the pool next."

"That sounds sensible," said Honey. "There are lots of places in the rocks where the bottles could be hidden."

As the five fairies flew to the middle of the island, Buttercup felt glad Rosa was

taking charge. She always knew what to
do in difficult situations. They soon got
to work searching among the rocks that
surrounded the beautiful pool – although
even the pool didn't look so lovely
now the sun's rays had disappeared. The
glittering turquoise water had turned to
a dull dark blue, and the drooping palm

trees had shed some of their leaves into the water.

Violet shivered as she darted in and out of the rocks. She was glad she'd put on her palm-leaf cape today. It was so cold on the island now!

Rosa had suggested that they search different areas around the pool, but it wasn't long before the fairies came together again, shaking their heads – no one had found anything at all.

"Perhaps we should go back to the castle," said Honey. She felt bad that her friends were spending their holiday searching for the sunshine when they should have been having fun!

But Rosa wanted to carry on. "No, let's go and check the waterfall," she said, feeling more determined than ever to find the missing bottles of sunshine. "I know that lots of sand fairies have already looked there, but there's no harm in us trying too."

Bluebell was worried they'd find the waterfall no longer running, but to her relief the water still gushed over the high ledge, although it didn't look quite so magical without the sun shining on it.

"I'm really thirsty," said Honey. "Let's have a drink while we're here." She fluttered down to the banks of the river. "Mmm, it's fizz-berry-and-banana shake today!"

"What do you mean?" Violet asked. What *was* Honey talking about?

The fairy princesses flew over to Honey, who was cupping her hands into the fast-flowing water that poured from the waterfall.

Honey looked over her shoulder at her

friends. "Come on, you've got to try it!"

The missing sunshine forgotten for
a moment, the fairy princesses rushed
over to join Honey, lying alongside one
another on the bank and using their
hands to bring up water from the river.

Sure enough, when Buttercup trickled
some of the liquid into her mouth, it
tasted of the ripest, fizziest berries mixed
with sweet banana. Yum, yum, yum!

When she'd finished drinking, Honey sat back on her heels and watched her friends sip at the water. "It's a different flavour every day – you never know what you might get!" But her smile quickly disappeared. "It's not looking good, is it?" she said, glancing around at the sand fairies who were flitting about behind the waterfall and shaking their heads. "Maybe we'll have to get used to cold, grey weather."

"But we can't give up yet!" said Rosa. "We've *got* to find the sunshine. This is the happiest place in fairyland – and everyone is *always* smiling. . ."

"Well, not *everyone*," said Honey.

"What do you mean?" Violet asked.

"Rosa's right, the island is a very happy place, but there is one grumpy sand fairy here. She lives in the shadowy sand dunes on the other side of the island, all by herself.

It's silly, but I've always been a bit afraid of her, although everyone says she's harmless."

"Wait," said Bluebell, pulling at one of her ears in thought. "Could *she* have stolen the sunshine?"

"Oh, I don't think so," said Honey with a wave of her hand. "This fairy *hates* sunshine — that's why she lives in the shadows of the sand dunes!"

Violet jumped up. "But if we've looked everywhere else, perhaps it's worth a try?"

Rosa was nodding. "Yes, I think so too! And we really want to help you. Honey, will you show us the way?"

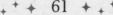

Chapter 7

The five fairies set off, flying up and over the rushing waterfall with Honey leading. Without the sunshine, it was already rather cool on the island, but as they flew, it suddenly got a LOT colder. Bluebell rubbed her arms to keep warm and Violet wrapped her palm-leaf cape more tightly around her.

At last they came to land on the shore, just in front of several high sand dunes.

The sharp hills of sand lined up along the beach cast shadows over the fairies – this place didn't look very inviting at all!

Violet was already setting off towards the dunes. She looked behind when she realized that the others hadn't followed her. "Let's find this grumpy fairy, shall we?" she said. "Even if she hasn't got the sunshine, maybe she has an idea where it is!" But her friends were all staring at the sand dunes as if they hid monsters, or the Pixlins from fairy tales.

"Perhaps we could persuade her to come out here instead?" Rosa suggested.

"I don't think that will work," said Violet. "Honey said this fairy likes to be left alone. But we really need to find her, and I can't do this by myself – I need your help. Please?"

"Violet's right," Bluebell said quietly. "As much as I don't want to go in there, it'd be much better if we all went to find her." She held hands with Honey and Buttercup, and together with Rosa they fluttered across the sand to join Violet.

"I think she might live in here," said Violet, pointing to a little gap between

two of the giant dunes. Next to it stood
a little sign which read: KEEP OUT!

Rosa peered in. Sure enough, there
seemed to be a tiny tunnel-like gap in
the dunes which led away into darkness.

"I'll go first," Violet offered.

The other fairies admired how brave
Violet was as she got down on her hands
and knees and crawled into the opening,
squeezing her wings tightly shut so she
could fit in the narrow tunnel.

Rosa took a deep breath and followed
her, then came Bluebell, Buttercup and
Honey. Inside the sand tunnel, it was dark
and damp. *What a horrible place to live*,
thought Rosa. *Why would anyone want
this as a home?*

"Wait – what's that noise?" asked
Buttercup, cupping her hand behind her
ear in an effort to hear better.

The others listened carefully too. Buttercup was right – there was definitely some kind of sound coming from inside the tunnel.

Violet crept further inside. Now she could hear the noise more clearly, and tried to make out the words.

"Twelve, thirteen, fourteen, fifteen. . ."

Violet turned back to her friends,

confused. "Er, I think it's someone counting?" She paused. "Yes, they're definitely counting numbers. . ."

"Twenty-one, twenty-two, twenty-three, twenty-four. . ."

Violet edged along the sand tunnel, but froze when she glimpsed a fairy in the darkness. It was gloomy, but Violet could make out the figure, because she was lit up by the gleaming bottles of sunshine lined up in front of her!

Chapter 8

"Who's there!" the sand fairy shouted. "Oh fairy-rats. Now I've forgotten what number I got to!"

Violet crawled further towards the sand fairy. The tunnel had opened up, and she soon found that she could stand once more. She shook out her wings and gave the fairy a little wave.

"Um, hello, I'm Violet," she began.

"I'm not sure what you're doing with the sunshine, but we really need it back."

Encouraged by Violet's bravery, Rosa spoke up too. "You see, Shimmer Island is all horrible and grey without it – and everyone is miserable—"

"Well, why should the other fairies be happy when I'm stuck in here feeling sad all the time?" the sand fairy protested.

"What do you mean?" Bluebell asked gently. "You can tell us – we promise we won't be angry."

The sand fairy bowed her head. "I stole the bottles of sunshine," she mumbled, "because I wanted everyone to feel as unhappy as me for a change!"

Honey had come to the front of the group and reached out her arms to the miserable fairy. "But why do you feel so bad?" she asked. "Why do you hide yourself in here?"

"It's OK for you!" the sand fairy replied. "You're so pretty, with your perfect long blonde hair. But look at this – who would want to be friends with an ugly fairy like me?" She took a step closer to the sunshine-filled bottles and was suddenly lit up by the rays.

"Oh wow!" said Violet, staggering back in surprise. "But you're beautiful!"

The sand fairy had waves of curly purple hair that stretched down to her waist, and big hazel eyes framed by long dark lashes. She wore a seaweed-pleated skirt and matching halter-neck top, with delicate bangles of shells on both wrists. "I know you're only saying that!" she said in a trembling voice. "All the other sand fairies are gorgeous and blonde – and I've got this stupid purple hair!"

Buttercup was shocked to think that the fairy had hidden herself away because she thought she was ugly. It was so sad.

Rosa had an idea. "How about we step into the light too?" she said. "I want to show you something."

"I suppose that's

OK," the sand fairy replied, her voice still shaky.

Rosa nudged her friends and they crowded closer to the sand fairy and the bottles.

As they were lit up by the sunshine, the sand fairy let out a little gasp. "Oh, but you all look different too!"

"Well, it would be a bit boring if we were all the same," said Bluebell.

"And I'd give *anything* to have purple hair," said Violet.

The other fairies giggled. They weren't surprised by that!

"Please will you come and join the rest of the sand fairies?" asked Honey. "I know they'll be happy to see you!"

The sand fairy gave a shy little smile. "Are you sure? I'm scared of what everyone will say. And they might be angry that I took the sunshine."

Honey put her arm around the sand fairy and gave her a gentle squeeze. "Please don't worry. We can return the bottles and make sure Shimmer Island is filled with sunshine once more," she said. "I promise everything will be fine. . ." She trailed off. "There's just one thing."

"What's that?" asked the sand fairy, a worried look on her face.

"If we're going to be friends, then you'll have to tell us your name." Honey grinned.

The sand fairy grinned back at her. "It's Coco."

"Oh, what a lovely name!" Bluebell exclaimed.

"Now let's get this sunshine back to where it belongs!" said Rosa, taking the lead as the fairies gathered the bottles in their arms and crawled back out along the sand tunnel.

A week later, the fashion fairy princesses were waking up for the final time in Honey's bedroom – it was the last day of their holiday on Shimmer Island. Bright rays of sun streamed in through Honey's diamond window, just as they had every day since Coco had returned the bottles of sunshine. The music of the songbirds, mixed with the sound of sand-fairy laughter, floated into the room every now and then. It was just one of the things they were going to miss so much when they were back in Sparkle City.

"This has been the best holiday ever!" said Rosa, as she dressed in a pink cloud-print playsuit. "I'm so glad you all came."

"Well, friends *have* to stick together!" Bluebell replied. She sat at Honey's dressing table, clipping a bird of paradise flower into the side of her brown bobbed hair.

"Honey, will we have time to go and say goodbye to Coco?" asked Violet.

"Of course," she said. "I think she'll be expecting you!"

Honey and the fashion fairy princesses soon found Coco outside her new coconut beach hut. She was fluttering about the glistening sand, playing coconut catch with her neighbour.

"Hi, Coco," said Rosa. "We're about to leave, but we wanted to come and say goodbye!"

"Oh, I'm really going to miss you!" said Coco. "You have to promise you'll come back and visit again soon."

"We promise!" Violet grinned. "But you have to come to Sparkle City too — we have so much to show you there!"

"I promise!" Coco replied. "Fairy friends for ever?"

The fashion fairy princesses nodded, blinking back tears. "Fairy friends for ever!" they called, and took turns to give their new friend a hug.

They were about to fly off when Coco suddenly raised her hands to her face. "Oh my fairyness! I almost forgot!" She ran inside the hut while the five friends waited outside on the deck, wondering what Coco had forgotten.

She emerged with her hands behind her back. "Can you close your eyes for a moment?"

Honey and the fashion fairy princesses did as they were told, and felt Coco hanging something around their necks.

"Now you can open them!"

Rosa quickly looked down. There,

hanging on a chain of plaited golden grasses, was a tiny glass bottle that burst with light. Rosa cupped it in her hands. It was the same size as the tip of her little finger, and it shone wildly. Was it really. . .

"Sunshine!" Violet cried, flying over to Coco and hugging her so tightly that the sand fairy's feet left the ground.

"You've made me so happy," said Coco. "I wanted to make gifts that give each of you a little bit of happiness every day."

"It's such a special present," said Bluebell, unable to take her eyes off the sunshine bottle pendant.

"And it's the perfect reminder of an amazing holiday," Rosa added.

The fashion fairy princesses all nodded in agreement. For this really had been the most incredible holiday ever!

If you enjoyed this

Fashion Fairy Princess

book then why not visit our
magical new website!

- Explore the enchanted world of the fashion fairy princesses
- Find out which fairy princess you are
- Download sparkly screensavers
- Make your own tiara
- Colour in your own picture frame and much more!

fashionfairyprincess.com

Turn the page for a sneak peek of the next
Fashion Fairy Princess adventure...

Chapter 1

Rosa fluttered into Bluebell's sky-blue bedroom, grinning. "Guess what's just arrived!" she cried, rushing over to where Bluebell sat on her enormous four-poster bed.

Bluebell had been doodling fashion designs, but she quickly pushed her sketchpad to one side. She looked up at her friend. "Oooh, is it my new blue silk beret? That was quick. I only ordered it yesterday!"

"No, but this is much more exciting," Rosa said with a shake of her long dark hair. "Look!" Rosa held out a peacock feather inscribed with gold:

To the Fashion Fairy Princesses,

You are cordially invited to tomorrow's Summer Ball at Dream Mountain.

Dress in your best outfits.

Yours sincerely,

The Dream Fairies

"The Summer Ball!" said Bluebell. "We've never been before!" She bounced on her bed in excitement, then leapt up and grabbed Rosa by the hand. "Quick!" she cried. "Let's go and tell the others!"

Delicately fluttering their wings, Rosa and Bluebell flew along the white marble hallway and into Buttercup's wing of the fairy palace. Buttercup and Violet put down the cupcakes they'd been eating as they read the invitation.

"I can't believe it," Buttercup said quietly, holding up the feather to her yellow stained-glass window.

Violet peered over Buttercup's shoulder. "Is it really tomorrow?" she said, scanning the words once more.

"And we have to wear our best outfits!" Buttercup added.

All four fashion fairy princesses crowded round the invitation. "Oh my goodness," said Rosa, "we don't have long to prepare!"

The fairy princesses lived in Sparkle City. It was half a day's journey to Dream Mountain from there. They'd have to leave at noon tomorrow to get to the ball in time.

Bluebell reached for a lemon cupcake from Buttercup's sun-painted cake stand. The creamy lemon icing melted in her mouth. Cupcakes always helped calm her down. "So," she began, "what in fairyland shall we wear?"

The four best friends fell silent for a moment. It was a very good question. They had to look their best for the ball.

"We can wear our new diamond-heart tiaras," suggested Violet, ducking into Buttercup's fly-in wardrobe. "The ones Fern made us." Fern was one of their best friends, although she didn't live in Sparkle City, but nearby, in Star Valley.

"But we don't have any ball gowns,"

said Buttercup. "What will we do?"

Rosa put her arms around her three friends. "We'll go shopping, of course! If we hurry, we'll get to Topaz's shop before it shuts." And in the blink of an eye, the four fairy princesses had fluttered out of Buttercup's bedroom and flown down the grand glass staircase of Glimmershine Palace.

Bluebell, Violet, Rosa and Buttercup arrived at Sparkle Sensations just in time.

"You're in luck — I was about to close," said the owner, Topaz, as they flew through the door to the clothes shop. "What are you looking for, fairy princesses?"

"Those!" all four friends shouted at the same time. They were pointing at the four beautiful sparkling ball gowns that were displayed on mannequins in the shop window. The dresses were identical, apart from the colour. The bottom of each ball gown had tiers of shimmering fabric, with a satin bow in the middle and a halter-neck top covered in gems. What's more, the dresses were in blue, pink, yellow and purple – perfectly matching each of the fairies' wings!

"I ordered them in especially for you," said Topaz. "I'm so glad you like them!"

The fairy princesses quickly changed into the dresses and fluttered around the huge shop. Sparkle Sensations was filled with skirts, dresses, tops, trousers and shoes in every single colour of the rainbow, and the whole shop shone with gems and pearls. It was one of the fairy princesses' favourite places.

Bluebell flew back and forth in front of the floor-to-ceiling mirror. Sparkles danced from her dress as she moved. She was so excited she couldn't keep still! Now they had the perfect outfits for the Summer Ball. Except. . .

"Shoes!" said Rosa, spinning round in her pale pink dress. "We need some to match!"

"Oh yes," said Buttercup, putting a hand to her mouth. She looked down at her golden-yellow ball gown. "I don't think I have any to go with this dress."

Topaz held up a finger covered in glittering rings. "I have just the thing," she said. Topaz fluttered behind a glass door at the back of the shop. She reappeared carrying a teetering pile of boxes. The fairy princesses quickly flew over and each grabbed one before they fell.

Bluebell lifted the lid of her box and her heart leapt. Inside, nestled between layers of delicate tissue, were sparkling peep-toe shoes covered in tiny blue gems. They were gorgeous, and like nothing she'd ever worn before – and they fitted perfectly, too.

The four fashion fairy princesses stood in front of the mirror in their completed outfits, beaming from ear to ear. Violet did a little pirouette in her deep purple dress, surrounding her friends with sparkles. "Now we're ready for the ball!" she said.

Yes, they were – and Bluebell couldn't wait!

Use the stickers from these activity books to give
Honey a magical makeover on the following page.

And coming soon...